Treasury of Illustrated Classics™

Treasure Island

by
Robert Louis Stevenson

Adapted by
Barbara Green

Modern Publishing
A Division of Unisystems, Inc.
New York, New York 10022

Series UPC: 39360

Cover art by Marcel Laverdet

Contents

CHAPTER

1

A Fine Excitement
in a Quiet Country Life

I, Jim Hawkins, will write my tale. I will keep nothing back from you except the location of Treasure Island. I cannot tell you this because there are still treasures there to be found. My story begins long ago when my father was the innkeeper of the Admiral Benbow Inn. It was then that the old seaman with the terrible scar on his cheek first came to live under our roof.

I remember him as if it were yesterday. He was a big, heavy man. A pigtail fell over the shoulder of his dirty, blue coat. His hands were twisted, and he had black, broken nails. And that shiny, white scar— I shall never forget it!

He looked along the seacoast, and whistled to himself. Then, with a voice high and shaking, he broke out in an old sea song that he would sing so often after:

"Fifteen men on a dead man's chest—
Yo-ho-ho, and a bottle of rum!"

He was a silent man, but was used to being obeyed. We called him Captain. All day he hung about the cliffs with his

brass telescope. All evening he sat in the parlor by the fire, drinking strong rum and water. Every day he asked if there were any sailors who had gone by along the road. At first, we thought that he asked because he wanted company, but soon we began to see that he was afraid.

He promised me a silver fourpenny if I would keep watch for a seafaring man with one leg. How that one-legged sailor haunted my dreams! On stormy nights when the wind shook the four corners of the inn and the surf roared along the cove and up the cliff, he would appear with a thousand cruel expressions.

There were nights when the captain drank a lot more rum than his head could handle. Then he would sing his wild sea songs. Sometimes he would call for glasses for all and would force the trembling company to sing along. Often I would hear the house

shaking with "*Yo-ho-ho, and a bottle of rum*"—all the neighbors joining in with the fear of death upon them. Each would sing louder than the other to avoid an angry remark from the captain.

His stories were what frightened people most of all. Dreadful stories they were—about hanging, walking the plank, storms at sea, and wild deeds on the Spanish Main. He must have lived a life among some of the wickedest men upon the sea.

The people were scared, but looking

back upon it, it was a fine excitement in a quiet country life. He was a true "sea dog" and the sort of man who made seafaring so terrifying.

One day in January a stranger came. He had a nasty look, and I saw that he was missing two fingers on his left hand. "Is my mate Bill here?" he sneered. The captain looked as if he had seen a ghost.

"Black Dog!" he gasped.

CHAPTER

2

The Blind Beggar

It was on that January morning that the captain had awakened earlier than usual. He had gone down to the beach. His sword was swinging under his old, blue coat. His telescope was under his arm. It was so cold that his breath hung in the air like smoke.

On that clear, frosty day, Black Dog came to the inn. This was the first of the strange events that rid us, at last, of the captain.

"I'll have a glass of rum from this child here," said Black Dog to the captain, "and we will sit and talk like old shipmates."

When I came back with the rum, I found them seated at the table. They told me to go away. For a long time I did my best to listen, but could hear nothing. Then I heard the captain say, "No, no, no—and an end of it!"

All of a sudden there was a terrific outburst. Their voices were so loud that I felt certain that they could be heard a mile away. A chair and table fell over. A clash of swords followed. Then I heard a cry of pain. In the next instant, I saw Black Dog run past me in flight. The captain, with his sword flashing, ran right after him.

At the door, the captain raised his sword to aim one last blow—but he hit the signpost of the inn instead. To this day, you can still see where the sword struck. That blow was the last of the battle. Black Dog disappeared over the edge of the hill. I turned to the captain. His color was gray. Finally, he spoke. "Jim," said the captain, "rum."

He was not steady on his feet and he leaned against the wall.

"Are you hurt?" I cried.

"Rum," he said again. "I must get away from here. Rum. Rum, I say!"

I ran to fetch it. As I hurried, I heard a loud noise. Running back into the parlor,

I saw the captain lying on the floor. At the same moment, my mother, who had been alarmed by all the noise, came running downstairs to help me. We lifted the captain's head. He was breathing hard, and his face had a horrible color. I tried to put the rum down his throat—but his teeth were tightly shut. We were glad when the door opened and Dr. Livesey came in. He was on his way to visit my father.

"Oh, Doctor," we cried, "what shall we do? Where is he wounded?"

"Wounded? A fiddlestick's end!" said the doctor. "He's not wounded. The man has had a stroke. I must do what I can to save his worthless life."

Between us, and with much trouble, we carried him upstairs and laid him on his bed.

"He should lie where he is for a week. That is the best thing for him," said Dr. Livesey. "Another stroke is sure to kill him."

At noon, I stopped at the captain's door with cool drinks and medicines.

The captain said, "Black Dog is a bad one, but there are worse. If they give me the black spot, it is my old sea chest they are after. There is something in there from Captain Flint. I was his first mate."

"What is the black spot, Captain?" I asked. But the captain gave no answer.

My poor father had been ill all winter, and he died quite suddenly that evening. Because of our sorrow, planning the funeral, and all of the work of the inn that still had to be done, I hardly had time to think of the captain.

He came downstairs the next morning. No one dared to bother him. His temper was more violent than ever.

On the night before the funeral, the captain got drunk. It was shocking to hear him singing his ugly old sea-song in that sad house. As weak as he was, he still climbed up and down the stairs. He went from the parlor to the bar and back

again, sometimes putting his nose out-
doors to smell the sea. He had a frightful
way of laying his sword before him on the
table. But with all that, the captain would
mind his own business and seemed shut
up in his own thoughts.

On a chilly afternoon the day after the
funeral, I was standing by the inn door. I
saw someone coming slowly up the road.
It was a blind man, and he tapped before
him with a stick. Bent over and wearing a
tattered cloak with a hood, he looked like
a hunchback. Raising his voice in a
strange way, he spoke to the air in front of
him saying, "Will a kind friend tell a poor
blind man where he is?"

"You are at the Benbow Inn, my good man," said I.

"I hear a young voice," he said. "Give me your hand, my kind young friend, and lead me in."

I held out my hand and that horrible, soft-spoken, eyeless man gripped it like a vise. I was so surprised that I struggled to draw my hand away. But the blind man pulled me close with his strong grip.

CHAPTER 3

The Black Spot

He said, "Now boy, take me in to your captain."

"Sir," said I, "upon my word, I dare not."

"Oh! That's it!" he sneered. "Take me straight in or I'll break your arm."

As he spoke, he gave my arm such a twist that it made me cry out.

"Come now, march!" he ordered.

I never heard a voice so cruel and cold as that blind man's. I obeyed him at once. I walked straight through the inn door and into the hallway. I knew the sick old captain sat in the parlor dazed with rum. The blind man was right

behind me, holding me firmly with his iron fist. He leaned almost more weight on me than I could carry.

"Lead me straight up to him. When he sees me I want you to cry out, 'Here's a friend for you, Bill.' If you don't do this . . . "

He then gave my arm a terrible twist that nearly had me fainting. I was so terrified of that blind beggar that I forgot my terror of the captain. As I opened the parlor door, I cried out the words he had ordered.

The poor captain raised his eyes. With one look at the blind man, his face became pale. His mouth dropped open. He tried hard to raise himself up, but I do not believe that he had enough strength in his body to do so.

"Now Bill, sit where you are," said the blind man. "I can't see—but I can hear a *finger stirring*. Business is business. Hold out your left hand. Boy, take his left hand by the wrist. Then bring it near my right hand."

We both obeyed him instantly. I saw him pass something from his hand into the captain's.

"And now that's done," he said.

And with those words, he suddenly let go of me and, with incredible swiftness, he skipped out of the parlor and into the road. As I stood there, I could hear his stick go tap-tap-tapping into the distance.

It was some time before either one of us came to our senses. But finally, I let go of the captain's wrist, which I found myself still holding. He drew back his hand and looked hard into his palm.

"Ten o'clock!" the captain cried. "Six hours. We'll do them yet." He then sprang to his feet.

Just as he stood up, he swayed. Then he grabbed his throat and fell forward onto the floor. I ran to him at once, calling to my mother. My haste was in vain—the captain had been struck dead! It is a strange thing to understand, for I certainly had never liked the man, but lately I had begun to pity him. As soon as I saw that he was dead, I burst into a flood of tears. It was the second death I had known, and the sorrow of the first was still fresh in my heart.

I lost no time in telling my mother all that I knew. Perhaps I should have told her long before. The captain owed us money from his stay at the inn and it was surely due us.

But we could not stay at the house much longer; the very ticking of the clock frightened us. And, at any moment, Black Dog and his friends might arrive.

We stood alone in the house with the captain's dead body. My mother got a candle. On the floor, close to his hand, we saw a small, round piece of paper. It was blackened on one side. *This* was the black spot! On the other side was written, "You have till ten tonight."

"He has till ten, Mother," I said. Just as I said these words, our old clock began striking. This sudden noise shocked us— but we were grateful that it was only six o'clock. We found his key tied around his neck.

We left the captain where he lay and hurried upstairs to where his chest had stood since the day he'd arrived. It was like any seaman's chest on the outside, but once the lid was lifted, a strong smell of tobacco rose up from the inside. We saw a suit of very good clothes that had never been worn. Under that there were all kinds of things: an old Spanish watch, two fine pistols, some silver, a bag of money, and a package wrapped up tightly in oilcloth.

"I'll have what's due me, but not a penny more," said my mother. She began to count the money in the captain's bag. It took a long time, for the coins were all from different countries and were of different sizes.

When we were about halfway through, I suddenly put my hand upon her arm, for I had heard in the silent, frosty air a sound that brought shivers to my body—the tap-tapping of the blind man's stick upon the frozen road.

CHAPTER 4

Storming the Inn

The sound drew nearer and nearer. We sat there holding our breath. Then the stick struck sharply upon the inn door. We could hear the handle being turned. The bolt rattled as that awful man tried to enter the inn. Then there was a long silence. The tapping began once again. But to our joy, it slowly died away.

"Mother," I said, "take the whole of it and let's be going."

That the door was bolted must have seemed unusual to the blind man, but I was glad I had locked it. Still, my mother, frightened as she was, would not agree to

take a bit more of the money than what
was owed her. She also would not take
less. So she continued her count until a
low whistle sounded. That was enough—
more than enough—for both of us.

"I'll take what I *have*," she said
quickly.

"I'll take *this* to even our account," said
I, picking up the package from the chest.

We raced down the stairs, opened the
door, and made our escape. We had not

started a moment too soon. The fog that had hidden the inn from view was disappearing. The moon was shining clearly around us. It was only just around the tavern door that a bit of fog still hung about to cover the first few steps of our escape. We saw that beyond the bottom of the hill, we would come forth into the moonlight. I grasped my mother's hand tightly.

This was not all. We heard the sound of running footsteps coming toward us.

We had just made it to the little bridge near the inn when my mother said, "Jim, take the money and run on. I am

going to faint." This was certainly the end for both of us, I thought.

I helped her to the edge of the bank where, sure enough, she gave a sigh and fell on my shoulder. I do not know how I found the strength to do it, and I am afraid I did it roughly—but I managed to drag her a little way under the bridge. There we were partly hidden; and it was there that we had to stay—within earshot of the inn.

I crept back to the bank again and lay down behind a bush. From where I was,

I could see the inn. I had hardly been there a moment when some men arrived.

There were seven or eight of them. Their feet were beating out of time along the road. A man with a lantern was leading them.

Three men ran together. Through the mist I could see that the one in the middle was the blind beggar. At the next moment his voice showed me I was right.

"Down with the door!" he cried.

"Aye, aye, sir!" answered two or three of the others. Then a rush was made upon the inn.

I saw them wait. They spoke in low whispers, as if they were surprised to find that the door had already been opened, but the wait was brief. The blind man again gave his orders. His voice sounded louder and higher, as if he were filled with rage.

"In, in, in!" the blind man shouted.

I heard a voice shout from inside—"Bill's dead!" But the blind man swore at them. "Search him, you shirking lubbers, and get the chest," he cried.

I could hear their feet rattling up our stairs. The window of the captain's room opened with a shatter of broken glass. A man called, "Pew, they've been here before us. I can't find the map!"

"It's that boy," said Pew. "I wish I had put his eyes out. They *were* here—they had the door bolted when I tried it. Scatter, lads, and find them!"

Just then we again heard that same low whistle that had frightened us when my mother was counting the dead captain's money. I understood now that it was a warning signal telling of some danger.

"There's that whistle again," said one man. "Let's go."

"Scatter and look for them," cried Pew. "If only I had eyes!"

The men began to run. As they did so, the noise of horses could be heard. Almost at the same time came a pistol shot. The men ran in every direction

and, in no time, not a sign of them remained—except for Pew.

Pew was tapping up and down the road calling in vain for his friends. Some riders came at a gallop down the hill. Pew turned and, with a cry, rolled into a ditch. He was on his feet in a second, but being very confused, he fell right under the nearest of the oncoming horses. The rider tried to save him but the blind man fell onto his side and moved no more.

I soon saw that they were officers. I leaped up and called loudly to them. They said that they had heard of a strange ship moored at Kitt's Hole and were going to see whose it was. As for Pew, he was dead—stone dead.

My mother was brought back to the village and with a little cold water and smelling salts, she was soon back to good health. I went back to the inn. Everything was smashed, and I could see at once that we were ruined.

Mr. Dance and a few of the other officers rode as fast as they could to Kitt's Hole, but when they got there, the ship

was already under sail. He called for them to come back. A voice called back to him saying that he had better keep out of the moonlight or he would get some "lead in him." Then a bullet whizzed by his arm. Soon after that, the ship was gone.

"And that," said Mr. Dance, "is just about as good as nothing. They've gotten off clean. Only I'm glad I stomped upon Master Pew."

CHAPTER 5

The Map

I told Mr. Dance about the package that I had taken from the captain's chest, and that it was the same package that the blind man had been after. We agreed to ride to Dr. Livesey's to ask his advice. When we arrived, his maid told us that he was dining at the home of his friend, Squire Trelawney. We followed him there.

We were shown into the dining room where they sat eating. Mr. Dance told them his report. The doctor asked to see the package, which once belonged to Captain Flint. "Have you heard of this Flint?" asked the doctor.

"Heard of him!" said the squire. "He

was the most bloodthirsty pirate who ever sailed!"

"Supposing that I had some clue as to where Flint buried his treasure. Will that treasure amount to much?" asked the doctor.

"Amount, sir!" cried the squire. "It will amount to this: If that package gives us a clue as to where the treasure is, I will fit out a ship at Bristol. I'll take you as the ship's doctor and Jim Hawkins as cabin boy. I'll have that treasure if I must search for a year!"

The doctor opened the package and found a book and a map inside. The book was marked with crosses and numbers. The crosses stood for the names of the

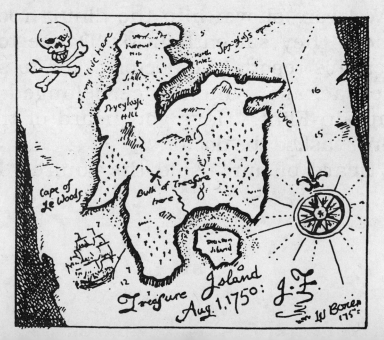

ships that had sunk. The numbers told of the captain's own share of the treasures that were stolen from the ships. The map showed an island marked with latitude and longitude. It was so clearly drawn that nothing more would be needed to bring a ship safely into harbor. The plan was set. We would find Flint's treasure.

I spent several weeks at the squire's house with Redruth, the gamekeeper. I would sit by the fire and spend hours looking over the map, dreaming of strange islands and adventures. Sometimes the island was full of savages with whom we fought. Sometimes it was filled with dangerous animals that hunted us.

The squire's letter finally arrived. He said that he had found a ship, the *Hispaniola*, and a sea cook named Long John Silver, who had lost a leg. With Silver's help, the squire had also hired a crew. The letter ended by telling me that I might spend a last night with my mother before Redruth and I set out for Bristol.

The next morning I went to the Admiral
Benbow Inn. My mother was in good
health and good spirits. And, thanks to
the squire, the inn had been repaired. The
squire had also found a boy to help my
mother while I was away.

The next day Redruth met me outside
the Royal George Inn where we took a

coach to Bristol. I slept the whole journey. When I opened my eyes, we were in front of a large bustling dock.

We walked along the docks to the inn where Squire Trelawney was staying. He came out to meet us, looking like a sea officer in his blue coat. There we saw a great many ships of all sizes, rigs, and nations. In some, sailors were singing as they worked. In others, there were men hanging on to ropes high above my head. The ropes seemed no thicker to me than a spider's web.

Though I had lived by the shore all of my life, I seemed never to have been near the sea until then. The smell of tar and salt was something new. I could not have been more delighted. My heart beat faster. Soon I would be on a ship bound for an unknown island—to seek buried treasure!

CHAPTER

6

Long John Silver

When I finished breakfast, Squire Trelawney gave me a note to take to Long John Silver at the sign of the Spyglass Inn. He said that I should easily find the place by following the docks and keeping a lookout for a little tavern with a large brass telescope on its sign. I gladly set off, happy at the chance to see some more of the ships and the seamen, now at their busiest.

I found the inn. It was a bright place with red curtains, and the sign was newly painted. In spite of the clouds of tobacco smoke, I could see inside. I found the customers to be mostly sailors. They

talked so loudly that I hung about the door, almost afraid to go in.

A man came out of the side room and, at a glance, I was sure that it must be Long John Silver. His left leg was cut off just above the knee. Under his left shoulder, he carried a crutch. He was tall, strong, and moved about like a bird among the tables. He had merry words for the more favored of his guests. I liked him right away. I plucked up my courage and walked over to where he stood talking. I stood there at his side until he took notice of me.

"Mr. Silver, sir?" I asked, holding out the note from Squire Trelawney.

"Yes, my lad," said he, "such is my name, to be sure. And who may you be?" Just then, he saw the squire's letter in my hand and said, "I see. You are our cabin

boy. Pleased I am to see you." He shook my hand firmly.

Now to tell you the truth, from the very first mention of Long John in the squire's letter, I had a fear in my mind that he might prove to be the very one-legged sailor for whom I had watched for so long at the Admiral Benbow. But one look at the man before me was enough. I had seen the captain, Black Dog, and the blind man, Pew. I knew what a pirate was like—and they were very different creatures from this clean and pleasant-tempered man.

As we stood there talking, one of the men at the far side of the room got up suddenly and ran for the door. He was out

in the street in a moment. I recognized him at once. It was the same man, missing two fingers, who had come first to the Admiral Benbow Inn.

"Oh," I cried, "stop him. It's Black Dog!"

"I don't care two coppers who he is," cried Silver. "He hasn't paid his bill. Run and catch him!"

One of the others, who was nearest the door, leaped up and started after him.

"Who did you say he was?" Silver asked. "Black *what*?"

"Dog, sir," said I. "Hasn't the squire told you about the pirates? He was one of them."

"In *my* house? Was that you drinking with him, Morgan? Step up here. You never set eyes on that Black Dog before, did you now?" Silver asked.

"Not I, sir," Morgan said with a salute.

"I don't know that name . . . ," said Silver. "Yet I think that I've seen that man before. He used to come in with a blind beggar."

"I know the blind man, too. His name was Pew," I said. "The man came back without Black Dog."

Silver said, "What's the squire to think now! I have this Black Dog sitting in my own house and drinking my own rum. Then you come and tell me of it—and I let

were sorry that Black Dog had gotten away, but we all agreed that there was nothing that could be done about it.

"All men on board by four this afternoon," shouted the squire. Silver took up his crutch to leave.

"Ayc, aye, sir," cried Silver as he passed through the door.

"Well, Squire," said Dr. Livesey, "this Silver suits me. And now, may Jim come on board with us?"

"To be sure, he may," said the squire. "Take your hat, Hawkins, and we'll see to the ship."

On this night we got ready to sail. The next day, we were off with the morning tide.

him give me the slip right before my eyes! But what could I do with this old timber I hobble on?" Silver sighed. We agreed to tell the squire the story.

On our walk along the dock, Silver made himself the most interesting companion. He told me about the different ships that we passed; he spoke about the work that was going on, how one ship was unloading, another taking in cargo, and a third getting ready for sea. Here was one of the best possible shipmates, I thought.

At the inn, Dr. Livesey and Squire Trelawney were seated together. Long John Silver told his story. The two men

CHAPTER 7

Conspiracy at Sea

All the crew liked Long John Silver. He had a way of talking to each man and doing everyone some service. He was always kind to me, and he always seemed glad to see me in the galley, which he kept neat as a new pin.

"Come in, Hawkins. There's nobody more welcome than yourself, my son. Here's Cap'n Flint—I calls my parrot Cap'n Flint after the famous buccaneer," said Silver.

The parrot would say, "Pieces of eight! Pieces of eight! Pieces of eight!" so quickly, you wondered why it wasn't out of breath.

In the meantime, the ship's captain, Captain Smollett, and the squire were not on friendly terms. Captain Smollett never spoke except when he was spoken to, and even then his answers were sharp. He had told the squire how unhappy he was at not having had the choice of his own crew.

Yet every man aboard seemed well content. That was as it should have been—for no crew was so spoiled since Noah put out to sea. Double portions of grog were usual, and there was plum pudding every other day. There was a barrel of apples, and anyone who wanted could take one.

Great good came of that apple barrel, as you shall see. If it had not been for the barrel, we would have had no warning— and might all have perished by the hand of treachery. This was how it came about.

It was the last day of our outward voyage. Before noon the next day, we should see Treasure Island.

We had a steady breeze and a quiet sea. Everyone was in the best of spirits because we were now so near the end of the first part of our adventure.

Just after sundown, when all my work was over, I decided that I'd like an apple. Captain Smollett was forward, looking out for the island; the man at the helm was watching the sail and whistling away gently to himself. That was the only sound except for the sea.

I climbed into the barrel and found all the apples gone. There I sat. The rocking

movement of the ship nearly put me to sleep when a heavy man sat down. The barrel shook as he leaned his shoulders against it. I was about to jump up when the man began to speak. I recognized the voice at once. It was Long John Silver.

Before I heard more than a dozen words, I realized that the lives of all the honest men on the *Hispaniola* depended upon me alone. Silver and his men were talking of mutiny!

Silver was telling the men about how he had sailed with the pirates Flint and Pew. He told the story about how on the same day he had lost his leg, Pew had lost his eyes.

"Here's what I say," Silver was saying, "you'll speak soft and stay sober till I

give the word. Squire Trelawney and the
doctor shall find the treasure for us. They
will help us get it on board, and then it is
our time."

"What will we do with them then?"
asked a sailor.

"Now there's a man for me," Silver said.
"Well, what do you think we should do,
my lads? Put 'em ashore? Cut 'em down
like so much pork? I give my vote—death!
When I'm a rich man, do you think I'd
want any of these men coming home?
Only one thing," Silver continued, "I claim
Trelawney. I'll wring his neck off his body
with these hands."

He turned to one of the young sailors and said, "Dick, get me an apple."

You may well imagine the terror I felt! I would have leaped out of the barrel right then and made a run for it, but my legs just wouldn't work. My heart seemed to have stopped right then. All of a sudden, I was saved by the voice of the lookout shouting, "Land ho!"

There was a great rush of feet across the deck, and I was able to slip out of my hiding place without being seen. I was just getting over the horrid fear of the last few moments when I heard Captain Smollett giving orders.

I hurried off to search for Squire Trelawney and Dr. Livesey. I had to tell them of Silver's plans. I found Dr. Livesey on the quarterdeck.

"Doctor," said I, "get the squire and the captain down to the cabin. I have some terrible news."

The three gentlemen went below. I waited for a minute, then I followed them.

"Now, Hawkins," said the squire, "if you have something to say, speak up."

I told the whole of Silver's speech. The three of them then began to discuss how many of the crew they could trust. They found that there were very few. We had only seven to match wits and strength against nineteen!

"Well, gentlemen," said the captain, "the best I can say is that we must try to keep a bright outlook."

Things looked bad, and I began to feel helpless. We all knew that we would come to blows with Silver's men before long. The three of them put their faith in me. Since the men were not shy with me, I could find out what was going on. Indeed, it was through me that safety had come this time.

In the meantime, there were only seven out of twenty-six on whom we knew we could count and one of those—myself—was only a boy.

CHAPTER

8

Jim Goes Ashore

I came on deck the next morning and looked at the island. I saw gray woods and rocky hills. Although it was a warm, bright day, my heart sank. You would have thought that anyone would have been glad to get onto land after having been at sea for so long, but I hated the very thought of Treasure Island. All I could think of was that, there, we'd have to fight Long John and his mutinous band.

We had a dreary morning's work ahead of us. There was no sign of a wind, and the boats had to be rowed from the ship to shore. The men all grumbled. Instead of keeping the crew in order, the sailor who was in command of my boat grumbled as loudly as the worst. We dropped anchor. Treasure Island was covered with woods, and I noticed the doctor sniffing like someone tasting a bad egg.

"I do not know about treasure," said the doctor, "but I am sure there is fever here."

Later, we held a meeting in the cabin. Captain Smollett decided that he would allow the men to go ashore. He did this to take their minds off the mutiny and to calm their anxious spirits. Those sailors must have thought that they would fall right over the treasure as soon as they landed. The captain's order was greeted

by a great cheer that echoed in a faraway hill and sent birds squawking around the ship.

Silver then took over. He made up a list of who would go ashore. Six fellows were to stay on board. The remaining thirteen, including Silver, headed for the island.

An idea then came into my head. It was the first of my ideas that were to save our lives. In a jiffy, I slipped into the nearest boat as it shoved off. No one noticed me. But Silver, from another boat, looked sharply over and called out to know if it was I. At that moment, I began to regret what I had done.

The boat I was in reached shore first.

"Jim, Jim!" I heard Silver shouting.

But I ran ahead till I could run no longer. I was so pleased to have given the slip to Long John that I began to enjoy myself. I looked around me with delight at the strange land I was in. I left my ship-mates behind, and nothing stood before me but animals and birds. A snake hissed at me. Little did I suppose that it was a deadly enemy—a rattlesnake.

Soon I heard voices. I recognized one to be Silver's. This put me in great fear, and I

crawled under cover. Silver and another member of the crew appeared.

"Silver," said the other man, "I would sooner lose my hand than not do my duty."

I then heard a horrible scream.

"In heaven's name," said the sailor, "what was that?"

"That?" said Silver smiling. "That? Oh, I think that is Allan."

"You've killed Allan, have you? Kill me too, if you can, but I defy you," said the sailor.

With that, this brave fellow turned his back on Silver and set off walking for the beach. With a cry, Silver whipped the crutch from under his arm. He sent it flying straight toward the sailor's back. It

struck with a shocking violence, right between the man's shoulders. His hands flew up, and he gave a short gasp and fell. Silver, crawling along the ground without his crutch yet still as quick as a monkey, was on top of him in an instant. He buried his knife into that poor man's body.

I do not know what it is to faint, but I do know that for the next little while the whole world swam away from me in a mist. When I came to myself again, that monster, Silver, had put himself together, crutch under his arm and hat upon his head. He minded the dead man not at all, but was cleaning his bloodstained knife upon the grass. Nothing else was changed. I could scarcely believe that a murder had really been done—and right there in front of my eyes.

Then Silver put his hand into his pocket, brought out a whistle, and blew upon it. I could not be sure what that whistle blast meant but assumed that it summoned more men.

I ran as I had never run before. As I did so, fear grew within me until it turned into a kind of frenzy. When the gun fired for our return to the ship, how could I go among those fiends? The murder I had just seen filled me with dread.

All this I was thinking as I was running. Without taking any notice, I had come to the foot of a little hill that had two peaks. I was on a part of the island that looked like a forest. There were huge oak and pine trees around me. Here, a new alarm made me stop with a thumping heart.

My eyes turned in the direction of some falling stones. Then I saw a figure jump behind a tree. What it was, I could not tell. It was big and shaggy. Was it a bear? It appeared again from behind a tree, quick as a deer. It ran on two legs like a man—but unlike any man I had ever seen. The man hid behind another tree. He must have been watching me closely, for as soon as I began to move, he appeared again and took a step to meet me.

CHAPTER

9

The Island Dweller

To my wonder and confusion, he threw himself on his knees before me.

"Who are you?" I asked.

"Ben Gunn," he answered. "I am poor Ben Gunn, I am, and I haven't spoken to a man these three years."

I could now see that his face was almost pleasing, but his skin was burnt by the sun, and his lips were blackened. Of all the beggar men I have seen, he was the most ragged. His clothes were tattered and held together by bits of string and stick.

"Three years!" I cried. "Were you ship-wrecked?"

"Nay, mate—marooned," said he.

I had heard of the word, and I knew it stood for a horrible kind of punishment among pirates where a man is put ashore and left behind on some lonely island.

He continued, "I've lived on goats, berries, and oysters since then. Do you happen to have a piece of cheese about you? Many is the long night I've dreamed of cheese. What do you call yourself?"

"Jim," I told him.

All the time he was talking, he had been feeling the cloth of my jacket, smoothing my hand, and looking at my boots. He seemed to be showing a great delight in seeing a fellow creature.

"Jim," he went on, "I've lived rough. But here on this lonely island, I'm back to leading a good life." There came a shadow over his face, and he raised a finger as if to give me a warning.

"Jim, tell me, is that Flint's ship?" he asked.

At this, I had a happy thought. I began to believe that I had found a friend. I answered him at once.

"It's not Flint's ship. Flint is dead, but I will tell you that there are some of Flint's men aboard, worse luck for the rest of us.

"Not a sea cook with one leg?" he gasped.

"Silver?" I asked.

"Ah, Silver!" says he. "That was his name."

"He is the cook," I told him. I made up my mind that I would tell him the whole story of our voyage—and the trouble in which we found ourselves. He listened with great interest. When I had finished, he patted me on the head.

"You're a good lad, Jim. Will your squire want some help from me? I will help him for one thousand pounds."

He told me that he had been on Flint's ship when the treasure was buried by Flint and six of his sailors. A week later, only Flint returned. Ben went on to say that he had been on another ship three years later when the island was sighted once again. He'd told his crewmates about the treasure that Flint had buried. Their captain hadn't been pleased at this news, but had agreed to let them go ashore and look for the treasure.

For twelve days they searched and searched, but they had no luck. And each day they had a worse word for Ben Gunn. Then one morning, he said, they gave him a pickax, a shovel, and a gun. They told him that he could stay on the island and search for the treasure by himself.

"Well, Jim," he said, "I have been here ever since."

Just at that moment I heard a cannon shot.

"They have begun to fight!" I cried. "Follow me!"

I ran toward the ship. Close at my side trotted Ben Gunn in his goatskins.

"Left, left," said he, "keep to your left, mate Jim! Under the trees! There's where I killed my first goat. They don't come down here anymore for fear of Ben Gunn. There's the cemetery. I come here and pray—when I think a Sunday would be about due."

He kept talking as we ran, neither expecting nor getting any answer. I have no idea how long we ran until, without warning, we came in sight of a large wooden stockade.

It was at that moment that a cannonball came tearing through the trees and fell onto the ground near where we were standing. Ben ran in one direction. I ran in another. This time, my fleeing steps took me to the cove where the *Hispaniola* still lay. But to my surprise, the ship that had brought us to Treasure Island was now flying a pirate flag. As I looked, there was another flash and another shot from the ship. It was the last of the gunfire. Then I saw

that the flag of England was flying in the air above the stockade.

The flag told me that the squire and the doctor were alive and barricaded in the stockade. Not knowing what to do next, I walked back to the stockade, where I found myself once again with my friends.

How they had come to be there was told to me by Squire Trelawney. The doctor had gone ashore and found the stockade. When he'd returned to the ship, he convinced the squire and

Captain Smollett that the stockade would be the safest place for them to defend themselves against Long John Silver and his band of mutineers. The fence around the stockade would serve us well as protection. The stockade itself would shelter us from bad weather.

Both the squire and captain agreed. They had set off in two small boats with the squire's three servants, food, guns, and an honest sailor named Gray. Their trip had been dangerous. They'd been menaced by cannon fire from the ship as they made their way to shore.

CHAPTER 10

Every Man for Himself

The trip from the small boat to the stockade had not been without ill luck for our group. Redruth, the squire's loyal servant, had been felled by a shot. In their attempt to bring him to safety, the boat full of supplies had been lost to the evil pirates. Now, every man on Treasure Island had a gun.

This was the point at which I joined up once again with the squire and the doctor. All through the evening, the pirates kept thundering away with their newly found guns. Ball after ball flew over into the stockade, kicking up the sand. But they had to fire high to get it over the walls of the stockade, and the shot fell dead and buried itself into the soft sand. We soon got used to that sort of horseplay and minded it no more than we would have minded a cricket.

The pirates were seventeen men, but three of them were wounded. We had the lucky position of shelter inside the stockade—but we were only seven. Captain Smollett told us to be ready for an attack.

The captain was a wise man. He gave every man a job in the stockade. He went

around keeping up our spirits and lending a hand at whatever it was that had to be done.

Early the next morning, I was awakened by someone calling out, "Flag of truce!" I ran to look outside. It was Silver.

"Give us the chart to get the treasure. We'll offer you a choice: Either you come aboard with us after we have the treasure, and we'll see you safely ashore, or we'll divide the money and you'll stay here. I promise to send the first ship we sight to pick you up."

The captain said, "Now hear me. If you'll come up one by one—I'll clap you in irons and take you home to a fair trial in England. If you don't—I'll put a bullet in you the next time we meet! That's my answer to you, sir!"

Silver was angry now. He shook out the fire in his pipe and roared, "Before an hour's out, you'll be sorry for those words. Them that die will be the lucky ones!"

With that dreadful oath, he disappeared among the trees.

Soon the pirates attacked. They waved their swords and guns. From a safe distance, well out of harm's way, Silver was

urging them on. They swarmed over the stockade fence like monkeys. The squire and Gray fired again and again. Three men fell.

But four of them had made it, and they were now inside the stockade. In a moment, they were up the hill and upon us. The house was full of smoke. Cries were heard and pistol shots rang in my ears.

"Fight them in the open!" cried Smollett.

I grabbed a sword from the pile. At the same time, someone grabbed another and gave me a cut across the knuckles, which I hardly felt. Someone

else was close behind me, but I knew not whom. When I turned, I saw the doctor beating down his attacker—sending him sprawling upon his back with a great slash across his face.

With my sword raised, I ran around the corner of the stockade. At the next moment, I was face-to-face with one of the pirates. He roared aloud as his sword went above his head, flashing in the sunlight. When I tried to spring upon him, I missed my footing and rolled down a steep slope. In another moment, he would have cut me down without mercy. The squire saw what was happening. He shot. The pirate fell. I was saved.

Nothing remained of the attacking party except the five who had fallen dead—four on the inside of the stockade and one on the outside.

The doctor, Gray, and I ran for shelter. The fighting would begin again soon. We saw the price we had paid for our victory. One man—Hunter—lay wounded. Another was dead, shot through the head.

"Have they run?" asked Captain Smollett.

"All that could," said Dr. Livesey, "but there are five of them who will never run again!"

The pirates did not return—there wasn't even so much as another shot out of the woods. But sadly, Hunter never recovered. He suffered all day. The bones in his chest had been crushed by a blow, and he died that night.

After tending to the wounded among us, Dr. Livesey went off in search of Ben Gunn. I began washing out the blockhouse. Then I washed all the things from dinner. All the time, envy in me kept rising as I thought of the doctor walking in the cool shadows of the woods with the birds and the fresh smell of the pines about him.

Then I got an idea into my head. I would go off on my own. I took some biscuits, pistols, bullets, and powder. Before the others noticed, I was out of the stockade and into the thickest of the trees. I was on my way to the white rock where Ben Gunn told me his boat was hidden. The sun was beginning to set, and I saw that I had no time to lose if I were to get to the boat that evening.

I headed for the east coast of the island. There, I could not be seen from the ship. Cool breezes blew about me. After a few more steps, I came out into the open where I could see the blue sea stretching far to the horizon. The surf tumbled and tossed its foam along the beach. As I crept up on a ridge, I saw the *Hispaniola*, still flying a pirate flag. I sat down and decided to wait until darkness.

CHAPTER 11

Captain Jim

The sea was never quiet around Treasure Island. The air might be without a breeze, but the great waves would still crash along the shore. They thundered by day and by night. I don't think there is anyplace on the island where a person would be out of earshot of their noise.

It was becoming dark and quite foggy, yet I could still see the *Hispaniola* clearly. Alongside was one of the smaller boats. Silver was in it—I could always recognize him! The men in the boat were laughing and talking, but it was too far away to be able to hear what they were saying. Soon after, Silver's boat pulled out for the shore.

By this time, the sun had gone down, and I went to find Ben Gunn's boat. The white rock where he said he hid it was still a good distance away. Finally, in a hollow by the rock, I saw it. It was homemade—if ever anything were homemade. It had a lopsided frame of tough wood and upon that a covering of goatskin. It was very small, even for me. I guessed that it was the worst boat ever made, but for all that, I knew that it would serve my purpose.

With all of the sunlight gone, all that I could see was the fire around which the pirates sat on the shore and a mere blur coming through the foggy air. That blur was the *Hispaniola*, lighted at the stern window.

I had my plan, and it was this: I would slip out and cut the *Hispaniola* adrift. She would then go wherever the tide might take her. I picked up the small, light boat. I put it down on the surface of the water and got in.

The little boat was safe for a person of my weight, but it seemed to have a mind of its own. Do as I pleased, it would steer to the right when I wanted to go to the left. Turning round and round was the

trick at which it was best. It turned in every direction but the one in which I wanted to go!

I saw the faint outline of the *Hispaniola*. The bowsprit was soon over my head. I sprang to my feet and began pulling myself along onto the deck. I heard not a sound from the ship, and it gave me a strange feeling. I reached the end and swung my feet to the deck.

There I found Israel Hands and another sailor. Each was lying with a bottle of rum at his side. I saw splashes of dark blood around them. I felt sure that they had killed each other, but suddenly

Israel Hands turned his head and gave a low moan.

"Mr. Hands," I said bravely, "I have come aboard to take command. You will regard me as your captain."

He struggled to his feet. Seeing the guns at my side, he said slyly, "I reckon I've tried my last fling and lost. So I'll help you sail the ship where you want—*Captain Hawkins.*" He looked at me angrily and continued, "You cannot sail the ship if I don't help you. If you tie up my wound, I will help you."

"First of all," said I, "I can't have those colors flying. We must fly the Union Jack."

I pulled down the pirate flag and strung up the flag of England.

"God save the king!" I said, waving my cap. "And there's an end to Long John Silver!"

Hands watched me keenly. I was to take care of his wounds, and he would sail the *Hispaniola* to the North Inlet of Treasure Island. It seemed to me a fair bargain.

The next morning, we had the ship under way. The breeze served us well, and we skimmed like a bird. The coast of the island flashed by. The view changed at every moment. I was greatly pleased with my new command and also pleased with the bright sunshine. I had water and things to eat. Everything was going according to my plan. In short, I was happy with the great conquest I had made.

However, I was uneasy on board alone with Hands. His eyes followed me always as I moved about the deck. There was an odd smile on his face as he took the wheel. He craftily watched . . . and watched . . . and watched me.

We were sailing along fine when Hands said to me, "Jim, this brandy's too strong for my head. Be a good lad and run down for some wine."

I could tell that this was a trick. No doubt he wanted to get me off of the deck for some reason. Knowing this, I played along.

I went down the deck with a great clatter of my feet. Then I took off my shoes and crept back. I saw him take a knife and hide it in his clothes. This was all I needed to know—he now had a weapon! I then ran down to the galley and quickly grabbed a bottle of wine.

When I returned, Hands was just where I had left him. He called out orders as though nothing had happened.

"Now lad," he said, "look there. That's a fine place to bring a ship into. Stand by, boy. A little more starboard . . . now steady . . . a little larboard . . . steady, steady," he cried.

I was so interested in the way the ship was moving, that I quite forgot to watch Hands. Perhaps I saw his shadow or

heard a creak. But sure enough, when I looked—there was Hands. He was halfway toward me with a knife in his right hand. A savage look was on his face!

We both cried aloud when our eyes met. While mine was a cry of terror, his was the roar of a charging bull. I leaped sideways as quickly as I could. I let go of the tiller that I was holding to steer the *Hispaniola.* It sprang back sharply and hit Hands. He gasped loudly with pain and surprise. The knife he was holding dropped to the deck.

It was the tiller that saved my life, for it hit Hands with such force that it stopped him instantly. Before he could recover, I ran forward. I was safely out of the corner into which he had trapped me. I had the whole deck to dodge about. But as I turned, I saw that, once more, he was coming after me. I had to think carefully, yet quickly, what my next move would be.

CHAPTER 12

A Dangerous Proposition

I must stop here and tell you of the terrible danger I felt myself in. I realized the peril that faced me. There was one thing that I saw plainly—I must not get boxed in. I would then be like a sheep at the hands of a cruel butcher.

Wounded as he was, Hands moved very fast. His grizzled hair tumbled over his face as he came toward me. I drew my pistol, took a cool aim, and pulled the trigger. But there came no sound! The powder was wet with seawater! I cursed myself for being so careless! Why did I not reload my only weapons when I had a chance?

He was nearly upon me. I could feel
myself breathing my last breath of life.
Quickly, I placed my hands on the mast.
Seeing that I meant to dodge his attack,
Hands waited. We both stopped, studying
which way to move. I had often played at
home with friends in this way, but never,
you may be sure, with such a wildly beating heart.

Still, it was a boy's game, and I could
hold my own at it against an old, wounded seaman. As we stood facing each other,

the *Hispaniola* suddenly leaned to one side. We both staggered. Then the ship turned over to the other side. We both rolled together. My head came against his foot with a crack that made my teeth rattle. I had to find a new way of escape.

Hand over hand, I pulled myself onto the mast. Up so far away from Hands, I now had a moment to myself. I lost no time in charging both my pistols with gunpowder.

I could see that Hands had begun to see my better position, yet he put the knife between his teeth and began to climb up to where I was.

"One more step, Mr. Hands," said I, "and I'll blow your brains out! Dead men don't bite, you know."

He stopped instantly. I could see by the way his face was moving that he was trying to think of what to do. He took the knife from between his teeth. "Jim," said he, "I guess this is the end. It comes hard for a master seaman to kill a youngster like you."

I was listening to his words, when back went his right hand. Something sailed

through the air like an arrow—his knife. Suddenly, I felt a stinging pain. There I was, pinned by my shoulder to the mast. In that moment of pain and surprise, my pistols went off and fell out of my hands. One of the bullets hit. With a choked cry, Hands lost his grip on the mast and plunged headfirst into the water.

I began to feel sick and faint. There was blood on my shirt, and my shoulder burned like a hot iron. I held on to the mast till my fingers ached. The thought of pulling the knife out made me shudder, but it was this shudder that did the job. The knife had only nicked me and pinned my shirt to the mast. That little shudder broke me away, and I came to my senses. I went below and did what I could for my wounded arm.

I took the sails down with difficulty, then I looked over the side. The water seemed shallow enough, so I let myself drop overboard. The water barely reached my waist. The sand was firm beneath my feet, and I waded ashore. At about the same time, the sun went down. The breeze whistled among the tossing pines.

The moon's brightness helped me find my way to the stockade. I did not want them to mistake me for the enemy, so I crawled to the door on my hands and knees. All was dark within, and the only noise I heard was that of men snoring.

My foot struck something—it was a sleeper's leg. He turned in his sleep. He groaned, but I did not awaken him. Then all of a sudden a shrill voice pierced the darkness:

"Pieces of eight! Pieces of eight! Pieces of eight!"

It was Silver's parrot—Cap'n Flint! I turned to run. I struck against one person and ran full speed into the arms of another. He held me tightly. There was no way to escape!

"Who goes? Bring me a torch." It was Silver's voice.

One of the pirates left and returned

with a lighted torch. Thus my capture was made.

The glare of the torch lit up the stockade. It showed me that the worst of my fears was true. There were six pirates left—but no sign of any prisoners. I thought that my friends must all be dead! The parrot sat upon Long John Silver's shoulder. By the light of the torch, Silver leered down at me.

"So," said he, "Jim Hawkins has dropped in. Well shiver my timbers! I take that as real friendly."

I made no answer, standing there looking Silver in the face. I appeared brave enough, but I had black despair in my heart. Silver took a puff on his pipe.

"I've always liked you," he said, "and I'm going to give you a chance to join us. No one's pressing you . . ."

"If I have to choose, I have a right to know what's what," I said. "Why are you here, and where are my friends?"

Silver told me that Dr. Livesey had come yesterday with a flag of truce. The boat was gone by that time, and the

pirates had lost their advantage. Silver told me that my friends had then left the stockade. Where they went, he did not know.

I told them that it was I who had cut the boat adrift and killed the men on board. I had the boat stashed safely where they'd never find it. "I'm no fool," I said, "but I've seen too many die. If you spare me, I will save you all and take you from this island."

"Enough of this!" cried one of the pirates. He sprang toward me with his knife. "I say do away with him and let's be done with it!"

"I'll teach you better!" Silver roared at him. "Do any of you gentlemen want to have it out with me?"

Not a man stirred. Not a man answered.

"I'm captain because I'm the best man by a long sea mile. I like that boy. Let me see the man who would lay a hand on him!" said Silver.

There were whispers among the pirates. Then one of them stepped forward.

"This crew has rights like other crews," he said.

One by one, they marched out and left us alone.

"Now look here, Jim Hawkins," he began. "You're within a half a plank of death, but I'll stand by you. I'll save your life, and you'll save me from swinging." He continued, "I am on the squire's side now, lad. My men are holding a meeting now to see if they can rid themselves of me."

"What I can do, I'll do," said I. I knew it was my best chance of saving my life.

A short time later, the pirates came back inside. A man came forward and put a piece of paper into Long John's hand. He looked at it. It was the black spot! No one said a word. Finally, one of the crew members spoke up.

"We will no more call you Captain. You have ruined us. The ship is gone. You have let the squire and his lot go free. And then there's this boy, here."

"Is that all?" asked Silver, quietly puffing

his pipe. "Look here," the old pirate said, "if we kill this boy, you'll never get the doctor to come and see you every day to fix up your broken bones. As for the squire and his lot . . . look around you. Who cares where they are! You have meat and drink and plenty of warm places around the fire in this stockade. Would you want to change places with them?"

I could see by the faces around me that his words were not said in vain. The crew were listening. They were being won over to Silver's side. Long John sat there smoking his pipe.

Just then, Silver threw a paper upon the floor. We all crowded around to see what it was. I could hardly believe what I saw. It was that very map that I had taken from the sea chest of the poor captain!

CHAPTER 13

The Hunt Begins

How Silver had gotten this map, I could not understand. The pirates leaped upon it as a cat would leap upon a mouse. They passed it around.

"That's Flint's map, sure enough," said one.

Silver leaned back against the wall. A look of victory was on his face. "Choose whom you please to be your captain now," said he. "I'm done with it, by thunder."

They all cried, "Silver forever! Silver for captain!"

"Here, Jim—here's something for you," said Silver as he tossed me the paper the pirates had given him. It was a

small, round piece of paper torn from a
Bible. The printed side had been blackened with ash to mark the black spot. It
began to come off on my fingers.

I have that bit of paper here beside me
now as I write this tale, but not a bit of
writing appears on it anymore. There is
only what looks to be a scratch upon it.

That was the end of the night's business. Soon after that, we lay down to
sleep. But it was a long time before I
could close my eyes. So much had happened that day, and I had so much to
think over. Even though I was with the
pirates, I was safe now. Yet just that
afternoon, what danger I had been in.

Then I thought about Silver and all the
tricks he was playing. He was keeping

the pirates together and on his side, too. Yet all the while, he was just trying to save his own miserable life.

I looked over at him. He slept peacefully and snored very loudly. It seemed surprising that he was able to sleep, having so many enemies and so much danger around him.

That was how we all spent the night. The next morning we were awakened by a voice calling to us from the woods, "Blockhouse, ahoy! Here's the doctor."

Everyone shook sleep from their bodies. I could see the watchman arise from where he had fallen asleep against the door.

"You, Doctor! Top o' the morning to you, sir!" cried Silver. He was beaming with good nature. "George, shake up your timbers, son, and help Dr. Livesey over the side. All's well with your patients, Doctor."

Although I was glad to see him, I was ashamed to look him in the face. He would see me with the pirates and think I had joined them.

"As you see," Silver said, "we have a little stranger here. Slept like a log, he did, right alongside of John—stem to stem we was, all night."

"Not Jim?"

"The very same Jim as ever was," said Silver.

Dr. Livesey looked shocked. He

entered the blockhouse and began his work tending to the sick. The men treated him like the ship's doctor—just as if nothing had happened between them. They took his medicines like school children, not like the bloodthirsty pirates that they were.

When the doctor finished, Silver said to me, "Will you give your word that you will not give me the slip?" I gave him my pledge.

"Then, Doctor," said Silver, "you just step outside, and I'll bring the boy out to you. You must have a lot to talk about."

The three of us all went outside. Then Silver left us and sat down upon a tree stump. "So Jim," began the doctor, "I cannot find it in my heart to blame you, but heaven knows why you ran off."

I began to cry. I said, "Doctor, I have blamed myself enough. What I fear most is being tortured."

"Jim," the doctor said, "let's run for it."

"But I gave Silver my word. I cannot

go back on my word, but let me tell you that the ship is in the North Inlet."

Quickly, I told him of all my adventures. He heard me in silence. When I was done, he said, "There is a kind of fate in this. At every step, it has been you who has saved our lives. You found out about the plot against us, and you found Ben Gunn. And now, you've gotten the ship for us."

He led me back to Silver.

"Silver," said Dr. Livesey, "let me give you some advice. Don't be in any great

hurry after that treasure . . . and look out for storms when you find it. I have no right to say more, but I will say this—if we are both alive at the end of this adventure, I will do my best to save you from being hanged when we get back to England."

Silver's face glowed. "You couldn't say more, sir—not if you were my mother," cried Silver.

"Here's my second piece of advice," said Dr. Livesey. "Keep the boy close beside you and, when you need help, I'll be there to seek it for you. Take good care of Jim Hawkins. The devil take you if you don't! Good-bye, Jim."

Dr. Livesey shook hands with me through the stockade, nodded to Silver, and set forth at a fast pace into the woods.

One of the pirates called to us that breakfast was ready. After we finished, we set forth on our hunt for the treasure. We would have seemed a strange group— if anyone had been there to see us—all in

soiled clothes and everyone but me armed. Silver had two guns, the great sword he wore at his waist, and a pistol in each pocket of his square-tailed coat. There was Cap'n Flint upon his shoulder, babbling odds and ends of sea-talk nonsense. I had a rope around my waist and followed after him like a dancing bear.

At first, the growth of plants under our feet slowed us down. Little by little the hill began to get steeper, and the ground became stony. It was a pleasant portion of the island. We had not gone more than half a mile when we heard one of the pirates in front cry out with terror. We all ran to him as fast as we could. What we found there gave us all a start. At the foot of a big pine, a human skeleton lay on the ground. I believe a chill struck at every man's heart. Not a man among us said a word. Finally, Silver spoke.

"I have an idea," said Silver. "Use the compass to take a bearing along the line of them bones."

It was done. The legs pointed straight in the direction of the treasure. The compass read east-southeast by east.

"Make no mistake," cried Silver, "this is one of Flint's jokes. Don't it make me feel cold inside. He killed this man—one of his own crewmen—and laid him down here like a compass to show the way! Shiver me timbers!"

We started on our way again, but this time the pirates kept close together and spoke with low voices. The terror of the dead man had made their spirits fall.

We climbed higher and higher. Just as the map said, we could see all of the island. Right above us rose Spyglass Hill. Silver took more bearings with his compass.

"It will be child's play to find the treasure now," said Silver.

The pirates whispered among themselves. All around us was the silence of the woods.

All of a sudden from the trees in front of us, a thin, high voice struck up the well-known song:

"Fifteen men on a dead man's chest—
Yo-ho-ho, and a bottle of rum!"

"It's the ghost of Flint," one man said. He trembled as he spoke.

We were frightened.

Long after the voice had stopped, the pirates stared in silence. Their eyes were full of terror.

"It sounds *almost* like Flint's voice," said Silver. "But it sounded more like—Ben Gunn's. By the powers—Ben Gunn!" he roared.

"Why nobody minds Ben Gunn, dead or alive. Nobody minds him," said another.

The pirates' spirits had come back. Their faces were alive with color once more. Soon, they were chatting again. We headed toward the trees that were marked so clearly on the map.

CHAPTER 14

The Empty Hole

It was a fine walk upon the ridge where we found ourselves. The pines grew wide apart and there were large patches of sunlight between them. We grew nearer and nearer to Spyglass Hill. There were several tall trees on it.

The first of the trees was the wrong one. The second was wrong, too. The third rose up nearly two hundred feet into the air. It had a trunk as big as a house and a wide shadow into which all of us could have fit. The pirates' eyes burned in their heads as they approached the tree where the treasure would be.

Silver hobbled on his crutch and

cursed like a madman when the flies settled on his shiny, hot face. He took no pains to hide his thoughts; they were on his face for me to read as I would read a book.

With the nearness of the treasure, all his promises were forgotten. He was thinking that he would get the treasure and escape. He would cut every honest throat and then sail away with the riches. His promise to me and the doctor's warnings were things of the past.

"I'll not be beaten by man or devil," cried Silver. "If there's treasure here, I aim to lay my hands on it!"

Suddenly, not ten yards farther, we all stopped. A low cry was heard. Silver, who could not go as fast as the other men, doubled his pace. He dug away with the bottom of his crutch. The next moment, we had joined the others.

We saw a huge hole. It had been made some time ago, for I saw the side had fallen in and grass was growing on the bottom. There was a broken pick and several boards of broken packing cases. On one of these boards I saw the name

"Walrus." It had been branded into the wood with a hot iron. That was the name of Flint's ship. The treasure had been here, but now it was gone. Someone had found it before us!

Each of the six men looked as if he had been struck. But with Silver, the blow seemed to pass instantly. He kept calm and changed his plans in a split second. He looked at me wisely.

"Jim," he whispered, "take this and stand by for trouble." He passed me a pistol.

At the same time, he began moving and, in a few steps, he put the hole between us and the others. I couldn't help saying aloud, "So you've changed sides again."

There was no time for him to answer. The pirates, with loud cries, began to leap into the hole. They dug with their fingers, throwing the boards aside. Morgan found a piece of gold.

"Two pounds!" he cried to Silver, "That's your treasure, is it?" He passed it around to the others.

"Dig away, boys. You might find more," said Silver, laughing.

"Mates, do you hear that? That man there knew it all along!" cried an angry pirate.

"Is this all we're going to get for everything we've been through?" cried another.

They were all against Silver. They clawed the earth, pulling themselves out of the pit. They got out on the opposite side to where Silver and I were standing.

Well, we stood there—two on one side, five on the other. Silver never moved the whole time. He watched them, standing upright upon his crutch. He looked as cool as I had ever seen him. He was brave, make no mistake.

No sooner had I taken a breath, than a volley of shots rang out. Two of the pirates fell dead. I turned, and there was Dr. Livesey with Ben Gunn. The rest of the pirates took to their heels and ran.

"Forward!" cried the doctor, "Double quick, my lads. We must head 'em off at the boats."

At that moment, we were joined by faithful Gray.

We all set off at a great pace. We plunged through bushes that were sometimes as high as my chest. Silver was with us and kept up as well as he

could. As it was, he was already thirty yards behind us when we reached the edge of the slope.

"Doctor!" he called to us. "There's no hurry."

And indeed, there wasn't. We could see the three pirates running away from us and away from the boats as well.

So we four sat down to breathe. Long John, wiping his face, slowly caught up with us.

"Thanks kindly, Doctor," said Silver, sitting down. "You came in the nick of time for me and Hawkins, here."

Looking at Ben Gunn he said, "So it's you, Ben Gunn. You're a nice one, to be sure!"

"How de do," murmured Ben. He was wriggling like an eel. "How de do, Mr. Silver."

As we walked slowly down the hill to where the boats were, Ben Gunn told us his story. In it, he was the hero from beginning to end: Ben had wandered the island, had come upon the treasure, and had

dug it up. (It was his broken pick that lay at the bottom of the hole.) Then he had carried it back to his cave. It had taken him many trips back and forth until all of it was safely stored away.

The doctor had learned all of this from Ben. That is why he'd given the useless treasure map to Silver. Dr. Livesey explained to me that they had moved from the stockade to the hills in order to be clear of the sickness of malaria that lay in the swampy lowlands.

Ben Gunn had been sent out that morning to help me, I learned. When he'd seen the pirates, he had sung that sea song to frighten them. All my questions were now answered.

By the time all the stories had been told, and all the explanations were made, we were rested enough to continue on our journey to the boats. We finally got to the beach. There we found the two boats that had brought us to the island. The doctor smashed one so that the pirates could not use it.

We all got into the other boat and set out for the North Inlet. Soon, we passed around the southeast corner of the island. Three miles farther, just inside the mouth of the North Inlet, we saw the *Hispaniola*. The tide had lifted her, and she moved about freely by herself.

We were lucky that there had not been too much wind, or she would have drifted way out to sea and we never would have seen her again. Gray returned to the *Hispaniola* to stand watch.

We went to Ben Gunn's cave, where he had stored the treasure. There, to my amazement, I saw great heaps of coins and stacks of gold. I had never seen so much wealth in all of my life. It shone in that corner of his cave like a blinding light. This was Flint's treasure that we had come so far to find!

CHAPTER

15

Treasure and a Safe Trip Home

The squire met us at the cave. He was kind to me, saying nothing of my escape. He was polite and gave me neither praise nor blame. But at Silver's greeting, he became angry.

"John Silver," he said, "you are a villain! I am told that you are on our side now, but dead men hang about your neck like millstones."

"Thank you kindly, sir," replied Silver. He again raised his hand in greeting.

"I dare you to thank me!" cried the squire.

The cave was an airy place. It had a

pool of water with ferns growing around it. Before a big fire lay Captain Smollett.

"Come in, Jim," said the captain. "You're a good boy, but I don't think that you or I will go to sea again. Is that you, John Silver? What brings you here, man?"

"Come back to do my duty, sir," answered Silver.

"Ah!" said the captain, and that was all he said. I looked over at the treasure once more. That gold had cost the lives of seventeen men from the *Hispaniola*. How many more lives had been lost before that? Perhaps no man knew.

The men on Treasure Island had each taken a share in these crimes, yet each one hoped to reap the reward.

Here we all were, or what was left of us. Dr. Livesey, Squire Trelawney, and I were

all together again. After the heartfelt greetings we had given to one another, we all settled down to a hearty supper.

And what a supper it was—with all of my friends around me! Ben Gunn had made a salted goat. There was even an old bottle of wine from the *Hispaniola*. Never, I am sure, were people happier.

Silver was sitting way back, almost out of the light of the fire. He was eating heartily, quick to spring forward when anything was wanted. He even joined in our laughter. Silver seemed the same kind of helpful seaman as he had been on our voyage to Treasure Island.

After we feasted, we all went off to sleep. The next day would be a busy one.

We all knew how much work there was to be done. All the treasure that Ben Gunn had carefully brought to his cave would have to be loaded on board the *Hispaniola.* That was some job! But as for me, I slept more soundly that night than I had in some time.

The next morning, we were up early in order to begin our work. Gray and Ben Gunn went back and forth with the boat. The rest of us piled the treasure up on the beach.

It was a strange collection. There were a great number of coins from all over the world: English, French, Spanish, and Portuguese doubloons and double guineas. They were stamped with pictures of all the kings of Europe for the last hundred years.

Day after day this work went on. All the time that we were at our work, we heard nothing from the three pirates who were loose on the island.

On the third night of our work, the

doctor and I were walking on a hill above the beach. Out of the darkness below, we heard a noise that was half like crying and half singing.

"Heaven forgive them," said the doctor, "it is the pirates."

"All drunk, you may be sure," Silver said from behind us.

When we had finally finished loading the treasure and were about to set sail, we saw the three pirates. They were kneeling with their arms outstretched. It went to our hearts to leave them in this wretched state, but it was clear to us that we couldn't take them aboard and risk mutiny.

Suddenly, one of the pirates—I know not which one—leaped to his feet. With a hoarse cry, he drew his gun to his shoulder and sent a shot whistling through the air. It just missed Silver's head, hitting the mast instead. After that, we all kept under cover until we could no longer see those rascals.

That was the end of that. Before noon that day, to my great joy, Spyglass Hill on Treasure Island had sunk beyond my vision and disappeared into the round blue of the sea.

We were short on men aboard, so everyone had to take a hand in helping to sail the *Hispaniola*—all except Captain Smollett, that is. He was nearly recovered from his wounds, but still needed to rest quietly. He lay back on a mattress and called out his orders from this position.

We knew that we could not make the long trip back to England by ourselves, so we planned to stop and get a new crew for the rest of the journey home. It was just after sundown when we cast anchor in a beautiful gulf.

The doctor, squire, and I went ashore to spend the night. There we met the captain of an English man-of-war and spent such an agreeable time with him that the day was breaking when we arrived back at the *Hispaniola*.

Ben Gunn was on the deck alone. He had news for us: Silver was gone. He had escaped in a small boat. This was not all. He had not gone empty-handed. He had helped himself to a sack of coins worth, perhaps, three or four hundred guineas. I am sure that this helped him along on his wanderings!

Ben told us that he thought Silver had left to protect us. He said that if "the man with one leg" had stayed aboard, it would not have looked too good for us when we docked in England. Speaking for myself, I was very pleased to be rid of him at last, and I believe that everyone else felt the same way, too.

Well, to make a long story short, we got a few more men to help us sail home. The *Hispaniola* finally arrived in Bristol. We found out when we got there that they had thought we were lost. They were getting ready to send out a boat to come and search for us.

Only five of the men who had started out on the *Hispaniola* returned with her that day! Although a poor enough record, we were not so bad off as the other ship I have heard sung about:

With one man of her crew alive,
What put to sea with seventy-five.

Those of us who were lucky enough to have come back from Treasure Island had

a good share of the treasure. Some of us used it wisely; others spent it foolishly.

Captain Smollett is now retired from the sea.

As for Ben Gunn—he got his thousand pounds, and he spent it all, or lost it, in nineteen days! On the twentieth, he was back to begging again.

Of Silver, we have heard no more. That terrible seafaring man has gone out of my life. Perhaps he lives somewhere in comfort, for his chances of comfort in the other world are very small.

Whatever remains of treasure on that cursed island, I shall never know. But I do know that neither oxen nor ropes would take me back there again. The worst dreams that I ever have are when I imagine I can hear the surf booming about its coasts.

It is then that I awaken. I bolt upright in my bed, and I swear I can hear the sharp voice of Cap'n Flint ringing in my ears, "Pieces of eight! Pieces of eight! Pieces of eight!"

THE END

ABOUT THE AUTHOR

Robert Louis Stevenson was born in Edinburgh, Scotland, in 1850. He grew up a frail and sickly child.

His poor health later forced him to abandon a career in law. He then turned to writing and traveled around the world in search of a remedy for his ill condition.

In the four years between 1883 and 1887, Stevenson wrote his four longest and greatest novels: *Treasure Island*, *The Strange Case of Dr. Jekyll and Mr. Hyde*, *Kidnapped*, and *The Black Arrow*.

Stevenson spent his last years with his family on the South Pacific island of Samoa. There he continued to write until he died in 1894 at the age of forty-four.

Treasury of Illustrated Classics™